EXMOOR WRITERS
and their works

Volume One

Essays about nine writers, past
and present, who have described
Exmoor in fact and fiction

Victor Bonham-Carter

The Exmoor Press

First published 1987

ISBN 0 900131 55 1

MICROSTUDIES

Each Microstudy has been written by an expert or experts, and is designed to appeal to all who are interested in Exmoor.

The Editor of the Series is Victor Bonham-Carter

A list of all the titles is available from
The Exmoor Press Dulverton Somerset TA22 9EX

Printed in Great Britain by Williton Printers, Williton, Somerset, TA4 4QN

Contents

The source of each illustration, where known, is indicated on the relevant page.

Victor Bonham-Carter, editor of this Microstudy, is a professional historian, author of eight books and of numerous articles and scripts, including the two-volume history, *Authors by Profession*. He worked for the Society of Authors for 19 years, and was also Secretary of the Royal Literary Fund, the principal authors' charity, 1966-82. He is President of the Exmoor Society.

EXMOOR WRITING

Although I have written several books about the countryside and many articles and scripts, I do not regard myself as an Exmoor writer so much as an Exmoor editor. Having, in fact, edited or co-edited fifteen issues (so far) of the *Exmoor Review,* the annual magazine of the Exmoor Society, and 'mid-wifed' almost all the Microstudies published since Tim Burton and I started the Exmoor Press in 1969, I can truthfully say that I am well acquainted with Exmoor as a subject for authorship.

When I first came to West Somerset in 1947 to farm at Brushford on the southern edge of the National Park, I used occasionally to go browsing among Arthur Court's secondhand books in Dulverton. He had a mixed collection about Exmoor, most of the titles being about hunting—beginning of course with Charles Palk Collyns' *Notes on the Chase of the Wild Red Deer*; but, in among them, were comparative rarities such as Prebendary Hancock's scholarly histories of Dunster, Minehead, and Wiveliscombe, and other collector's items. I could have had the whole lot for a couple of hundred pounds, had I had the money and space, but I had neither in those days.

What struck me most forcibly, however, was that—although a handful of new publications appeared in the 1950s and 1960s—few of them were concerned with contemporary Exmoor, or the wider aspects of the region, other than sport, guide books, 'Lorna Doonery', and re-hashes of history. Hope Bourne's *Living on Exmoor (1963)* was an exception and, for me, it remains a classic; likewise Tim Burton's *Exmoor,* first published in 1952, re-written and expanded into four editions since 1969. This was the principal reason behind the venture into local publishing with the Exmoor Press, i.e. to provide readable worthwhile books of limited length (usually 64-80 pages), which we called 'Microstudies', on subjects such as archaeology, folk lore, places of worship, railways, moorland vegetation, rivers, forestry, and wild life. It was also the reason behind the publication of the *Exmoor Review*—first number edited and produced by John Goodland in 1959—and which, ever since, has deployed a marvellous array of articles, poems and pictures about almost every aspect of the National Park. A look at the Index* of the first 25 numbers of the *Review* proves the point.

The effect of these two publishing ventures has been threefold. First, it has enlarged and broadened the literature of Exmoor. Secondly, it has given many people—not necessarily writers by profession or even by inclination—the chance to contribute information or express ideas about Exmoor. Thirdly, and most importantly, it has strengthened and emphasised the *identity* of Exmoor as a region of great landscape

Withypool Common *Gibbs*

beauty, valuable wild life, interesting history, and a place where people live and work for their living—in short, possessing a character that has well merited the designation of National Park.

It was in considering these matters that I hatched the idea of writing essays about some of the writers, past and present, who have made important contributions to this sense of identity. The choice is mine and, to that extent, arbitrary; but I make no excuses, for the list speaks for itself. Noel Allen, naturalist and founder of the Exmoor Natural History Society. R. D. Blackmore, novelist, and Richard Jefferies, naturalist, each the author of a classic about Exmoor. Jack Hurley, who had a lifetime of experience as a local journalist. Hope Bourne, artist as well as author, the embodiment of wild Exmoor. Berta Lawrence, poet and historian, with a strong interest in the Brendons. Henry Williamson, naturalist and novelist, who lived just outside Exmoor, but too near to be excluded. Phoebe Rees, the blind dramatist and author of over fifty plays. And Leslie Wedlake, archaeologist and historian of Watchet, essentially an Exmoor port. Others will follow in a second volume, I trust, in due course.

VICTOR BONHAM-CARTER

*Available at £3.80 post paid from the Exmoor Society, Parish Rooms, Dulverton, TA22 9DP; or from Alcombe Books, 26 Alcombe Road, Minehead, TA24 6AZ.

Noel Allen *Frier*

NOEL VINCENT ALLEN

People who know Noel Allen, privately or professionally, will not be surprised to learn that he has written much of this essay himself, and that I—as the ostensible author of it—have no shame in quoting substantial sections in his own words, not merely because he has provided the essential information, but because he writes so easily and vividly: as indeed he has done on many occasions when contributing to the *Exmoor Review*, or when writing the Microstudies which I have published under the imprint of the Exmoor Press.

Noel was born on 23 December 1917, son of a farmer, in the Northamptonshire village of Titchmarsh, a small place then of about 500 souls overlooking the river Nene, and still largely self-supporting—with four general stores, a couple of bakers and butchers, three inns, two blacksmiths, a bootmaker, tailor, dressmaker, a variety of craftsmen, a coal merchant, and a carrier 'who transported goods and passengers in his horse-drawn wagonette'. No electricity or running water, most of the houses being thatched with rough stone walls. A car was a rarity and its appearance in the village a talking point. 'All the tradesmen had horse-traps for delivery, and pedlars with baskets of wares called at the houses and outlying farms'. Not much difference between the 1920s and fifty years earlier in rural Northants. 'So my youth', he writes, 'was entirely in and of the countryside'.

Every month had its season of activities for us village boys. Girls were rarely permitted to join in our pursuits. The year usually began with poling—floating poles down the flooded brook with all its twists and turns to the river a mile away; sledging when there was an inch or so of snow, and sliding on village ponds. Hoops were also a winter pastime, when a dozen or so of us raced through the streets to the cries and alarm of old ladies, cats, dogs, and hens. Much like motor bikes today! Tipcat, hopscotch, flying home-made kites, and marbles lasted only about two weeks, but bows and arrows which we made from willow and reeds tipped with pointed elder heads, usually had a much longer run in the springtime. A special activity in the Easter holidays was the construction from odds and ends of the 'boneshaker'—a primitive bike without tyres, brakes, pedals or saddle, which allowed a fair speed down hill though with considerable peril to rider and onlooker alike. It was our main means of transport.

Noel recalls too 'the longer days of summer' when he and his young friends were 'out and about on the farms and in the fields from morning to night'.

Fishing, bird nesting, and rabbiting, which called for considerable local knowledge and skill in dodging the three gamekeepers stationed around the village, plus the policeman. But we knew their movements far better than they knew ours, and though I recall several narrow escapes racing down a hedgeside with a keeper on the other, we were far too nimble to be caught. In the season we caught six or seven rabbits a week and sold them for a shilling each. At haytime and harvest we led the loaded carts and waggons from the fields to the stackyard, a regular job this for a shilling a day. In the evenings we took the great horses to the brook for a drink, then into the meadows for the night, after which we dashed to the river for a late swim. There was time for village cricket and football, and even rounders on occasions. Dandelion heads and cowslips were gathered for home-made wine, watercresses from the brook, moorhen and lapwing eggs for eating, blackberries for jam and pies, gleaning in the stubbles which kept the hens in corn for most of the winter, and early morning mushrooming. Plough Monday, April Fool's Day, May Day with a May queen, Oak-apple Day, Feast Days of the parish church, the maypole, the harvest home, the great bonfire on the fifth of November—all these were scrupulously observed. The days were never long enough, the holidays always too short.

At the age of eleven Noel won a scholarship to Kimbolton School where, for the first time, he had to tackle formidable subjects such as French and Latin, Algebra and Geometry, and—more agreeably—English and History. He was well taught and never forgot the grounding he got at school. Still a schoolboy, he became a village correspondent for the local weekly newspaper at half-a-crown per item—a good start for any writer, but the outbreak of war in 1939 put an end to any pretensions to authorship. Instead he joined the Royal Army Pay Corps and was posted to the ill-fated expedition sent to northern Norway, after Hitler had invaded that country in April 1940. Noel's unit landed on the Lofoten Islands and, as it was his job to pay the troops and settle bills incurred with the Norwegian civilians, he spent an exciting three months, travelling up and down the fjords and dodging bombs and gunfire right up to Narvik which—soon after its capture by the Allies—had to be evacuated. The return across the North Sea was no less dangerous, and Noel was lucky not to be sunk in one of the ships caught by the Germans, including the aircraft carrier, *HMS Glorious*, destroyed by the pocket battleships, *Scharnhorst* and *Gneisenau*.

Back in England Noel was sent to Ilfracombe where he remained for the next four years before a further posting overseas. He made the best of the opportunities offered by home service, by spending as much off-duty time as possible discovering the wildlife and exploring the countryside of North Devon. He had married shortly before going to Norway in 1940, and his wife, Marjorie, accompanied him regularly on his rambles, which provided him with the first chance of seeing Exmoor.

I lectured to the local Field Club, wrote short papers mainly on birds for magazines, also the bird section of *Ilfracombe Fauna and Flora*, a book of 266 pages published in 1946 and which remains the chief source book for the wildlife of North Devon. As the Field Club boundaries extended up to Heddon's Mouth, I made excursions into the western part of Exmoor. A regular walk on a full day off was from Ilfracombe to Lynton and a trip up Watersmeet before turning homewards.

Early in 1945 he was posted to the Middle East, first to Egypt, and then up to Jerusalem. Typically he wasted no time in broadening his knowledge of the natural history of the area, and with a small band of fellow officers explored almost the whole of Palestine and much of Jordan as well. Although German and other enemy troops had long left the country, political unrest was gaining momentum. The Jews were determined to oust the British, then the mandatory but—in their eyes—the occupying power; as a result, several of Noel's men were murdered or wounded by terrorists. He himself had an encounter when walking round Lake Galilee, when he was arrested by some armed Syrians, but was rescued by a detachment of the British-led Trans-Jordan Frontier Force.

> One of our most ambitious projects was travelling down the Dead Sea, landing a jeep at the southern end, and then going on down the great Wadi Ariba to Aquaba and the Red Sea. Mount Hermon, Kerak, Petra, Jerash, and Mount Sinai were all visited in those years, always travelling rough and sleeping in the open. As a Christian I found the Holy Land and the other 'biblical' countries fascinating, and ever since the Bible has been to me a living book.

After the war Marjorie joined him in Palestine, and together they built and ran homes and welfare centres for servicemen in Egypt, Cyprus and Jordan, working through a voluntary society known today as the Mission to Military Garrisons. Eventually they came back to England for good.

In 1968 Noel and Marjorie bought a house in Minehead and a year later settled in there. Shortly afterwards Noel purchased a small shop nearby and, having hundreds of spare books as well as some reference titles from a retired bookseller, he opened for business. 'Alcombe Books' has since become a household name for everyone in search of local, natural history, and secondhand books, and the business continues today in the charge of Caroline Giddens. The bookshop has also played an important part in the life of the Exmoor Natural History Society, founded by Noel in 1974 and now a thriving organisation with a membership in excess of 500 members, a Field Centre at Malmsmead and a Conservation Area and Nature Trail at Treborough. Noel has been chairman since the start and edits the *Exmoor Naturalist*, the Society's annual journal, to which he and Carol (now his assistant-editor) have contributed much of the reading matter, notably his surveys of the red deer, moorland birds, and butterflies, and her reports on plant life of the moor. These activities have strengthened the bond with the National Park Authority, Noel sitting on the Conservation, Deer, and Consultative Committees.

My own connection with Noel arose out of his activities as author and, in the first instance, of mine as editor (later co-editor) of the *Exmoor Review*, the annual magazine of the Exmoor Society. Noel began writing for the *Review* in 1971 and, since that issue, has contributed at least a dozen articles and reports mainly on birds and other wildlife subjects, but also a brief biographical account of E. W. Hendy of Porlock, author of *Wild Exmoor through the Year*, a survey of local sporting books, an account of James Gibbs, the miller of Codsend, and (with Carol Giddens) a description of Treborough Slate Quarry and Conservation Area referred to above.

Noel and I had first met in 1970 by an odd chance. In those days I travelled regularly by car to London and called *en route* on Norman Ogilvie, a friend who sold West Country and many other secondhand books at his home at Lower Ansford, Castle Cary. It was he who sold me an offprint of Noel's bird section of *Ilfracombe Fauna and Flora*, which led to my commissioning work for the *Review* and, specifically, one of the early Microstudies of the Exmoor Press, the publishing house launched by myself and Tim Burton in 1969-70. We published four titles by Noel: *The Birds of Exmoor* in 1971 (revised 1976); *The Exmoor Handbook and Gazetteer* in 1972 (revised 1973, 1974, 1979); *The Churches and Chapels of Exmoor* in 1974 (after Noel had put in two years of visits and research); and *The Waters of Exmoor* (which had involved him tramping 300 miles or so along and around the major rivers and reservoirs of the National Park).

He has also written several other books, and published some of them on his own account: *A Person from Porlock* (1978); *Exmoor Locations* (with Carol Giddens, 1982); *Birds in Exmoor National Park* (with Roger Butcher, 1984); two series of *Echoes from Exmoor* (1985); and *Exmoor Place-Names* (1986)—all these were published under the imprint of Alcombe Books. Quest Publications of South Molton issued his *Exmoor Wildlife* in 1979 (reprinted 1981). He also wrote the Preface to Carol Giddens' *Flowers of Exmoor* and has contributed to a number of other publications. The list is very long.

Finally, Noel as photographer and lecturer. He has taken and amassed a large number of colour photographs of excellent quality, of Exmoor. Some of them have appeared in the *Exmoor Review* and elsewhere, but their main function is to illustrate the numerous lectures he gives, and has given, under the auspices of the National Park Authority, amenity societies and educational organisations, but primarily at the West Somerset Community Education Centre in Minehead. Over fifty lectures and almost 200 conducted walks over Exmoor every year is a demanding programme for a man in his late 60s, not to mention preaching engagements and a heavy correspondence. However he declares 'I have no difficulty in keeping up with younger folk on moorland excursions, and can still readily spot the distant deer or lurking bird. All this for the love of Exmoor, and I trust for the love of God and men'.

RICHARD DODDRIDGE BLACKMORE

Richard Blackmore was not born in the West Country, but his family had been landowners and parsons in Devon for generations, and Blackmore is, of course, a well-known surname in and around Exmoor. Richard was born on 7 June 1825 at Longworth, a village between Faringdon and Oxford, where his father, John, was curate. Unhappily his mother, Ann, died within three months of his birth, and in the following year the Rev. John Blackmore accepted a curacy at Culmstock in East Devon. After re-marriage in 1831, John moved again, this time—in 1835—to Ashford near Barnstaple. It was probably due to these events that Richard spent much of his boyhood away from home—first, with his mother's sister in south Glamorgan, within sight of the Exmoor coast; and then on visits to his grandfather, another John, rector of Combe Martin and Oare, and to his uncle Richard, rector of Charles, south of Brayford. Exmoor and its environs were therefore in Richard's blood, and he strengthened the bond by going to school—following a family tradition—at Blundell's in Tiverton, and thence to Exeter College, Oxford, where he won a classical scholarship, graduating in 1847.

The early 1850s were memorable years for Richard. In 1852 he took his M.A. degree and was called to the Bar, and in 1853 he married Lucy Maguire, whom he had met on holiday in Jersey. Lucy was a Roman Catholic but later became an Anglican and, after initial parental disapproval, was welcomed into the Blackmore family. The marriage was a long and happy one, but unfortunately Lucy had delicate health and bore no children. She died in 1888. Richard also had his troubles. He was never able to practise as a barrister and was advised, on account of epileptic attacks, to adopt an outdoor life. This was not immediately possible but, after two years as a conveyancer and four or five as classics master at a school in Twickenham, fortune favoured him in the shape of a substantial legacy left him by his uncle, the Rev. Henry Knight, rector of Neath, and a bachelor, who died in 1857. This enabled Blackmore in 1858 to purchase a 16-acre plot at Teddington-on-Thames, build a house—Gomer House—in white brick, and start afresh as a market gardener. He lived at Teddington until his death in 1900, combining commercially unsuccessful horticulture with authorship which, but for a lucky chance, would also have proved a failure—despite his undoubted professionalism in both these vocations.

As a writer Richard—or R. D. Blackmore as he is usually known—had already ventured into poetry with four slender volumes between 1854 and 1860 and, in 1871, he produced a translation of Virgil's first two *Georgics,* but these were all done for 'pure love of the subject'. In

R. D. Blackmore

Richmond-upon-Thames Reference and Information Service

view, however, of the losses on the sale of his fruit and other produce at Covent Garden, he decided to turn his hand to fiction. 'Any ass can write novels, but to make a vine needs intellect', was his comment and, in a letter to an American friend later, 'All I make with the pen I cast away with the spade'. Indeed, towards the end of his life, he admitted that after some forty years as a fruit-grower he had only made an annual profit twice. His first novel, *Clara Vaughn,* published by Macmillan in 1864, was a story of Corsican vendetta, thick with murder and revenge and set in England; and—to quote from the article, *R. D. Blackmore's Other Books* by Cicely Cooper (*Exmoor Review* 1973)—it includes 'a romantic Manor House and a lovely Devonshire section at Heddon's Mouth'. However, although aimed deliberately at readers of sensational fiction of the kind made popular by Wilkie Collins and others, *Clara Vaughn* failed. Even so, following the success of Henry Kingsley's *Ravenshoe* serialised in *Macmillan's Magazine,* the publishers commissioned Blackmore to write a story in similar vein, suitable for a serial. The result was *Cradock Nowell* (1866), another richly romantic tale set, this time, in the New Forest. But the success of *Ravenshoe* was not repeated, and this led Macmillan's to refuse Blackmore's third novel—called *Lorna Doone.*

After the MS was completed in April 1868, it went the round of the magazine and book publishers until finally accepted by Sampson Low, Marston & Company in January 1869. *Two months later* it was on the bookstalls (compare that with today's production schedules!), as a 'three-decker', i.e. in three volumes as the custom was with novels in those days. By September it seemed to be going the same sad way as Blackmore's two earlier novels. Of the first 500 copies, only about 300 had been sold, the rest being remaindered for sale in Austalia. The situation was saved, however, by one wise move and one slice of luck. First, the publishers re-issued the book as a single volume in cheap edition. Secondly, the fact that publication in the new form happened to coincide with the engagement of Queen Victoria's fourth daughter, Princess Louise, to the Marquis of Lorne prompted a journalist to state that *Lorna Doone* was connected with the Marquis's ancestry. Quite untrue, but the public fell for it like a romantic schoolgirl falling in love with a prince! Mrs. Oliphant, the Scottish novelist, gave it a six-page review in *Blackwood's Magazine,* edition after edition was rushed out, and it is still selling today. It has been filmed several times, generally unsuccessfully, but more surprising—though no less incomprehensible—is the industry it has generated in the shape of tourist attractions in all their forms. Holiday accommodation, cafes, restaurants, shops, studios, and other varieties of business all cash in on the Doone story created by Blackmore, marketing a multiplicity of goods and services bearing the Doone trademark. In a recent report by a body calling itself the Exmoor Tourist Development Action Programme the idea of exploiting the 'Lorna Doone connection' for the mass market was given pride of place. Other considerations—such as the horrors of commercialisation—apart, it is an extraordinary development, arising—as it has—out of one novel published in 1869 and that only saved from extinction by a fluke.

Another by-product is the endless arguments about the precise location of the Doone Valley and its attendant features, e.g. the Doone Houses, the Water Slide, the window in Oare Church through which Carver Doone shot Lorna on her wedding day, and the Wizard's Slough where Carver met his doom. One prominent protagonist, Sir Atholl Oakeley, Bt., a former all-in wrestler, spent many years 'establishing the facts' and publishing the result of his researches in a popular booklet, many times reprinted—as indeed have other publications about Lorna and the Doones. Sir Atholl stated that in 1968 he convinced the Ordnance Survey—no less—that Lank Combe was the correct site of the Doone Valley. Thereafter, any writer who doubted this 'decision' was liable to receive a letter from Sir Atholl's solicitors on the grounds that alternative suggestions contravened the Trades Descriptions Act! However, no O.S. map pinpoints Lank Combe in that manner today. The principal fact to be gleaned from all this is that Blackmore deliberately romanticised places and people because he was writing a novel, not a guide book or a documentary, while also absorbing the tales about the Doones, current in North Devon when he was a boy and earlier. In his Microstudy, *The Lorna Doone Trail* (Exmoor Press 1975), S. H. Burton writes this:

> Whether the Doones ever existed or not is a complex issue, deserving (and frequently receiving) a book to itself. Here it is sufficient to say that Blackmore did not invent the Doone legends on which he based his book. From childhood he had been familiar with the many moorland versions of the Doone stories; familiar, too, with the various printed references to those vicious outlaws, one source of which (Thomas Henry Cooper's *Guide to Lynton)* pre-dated *Lorna Doone* by sixteen years. His own unquestioning acceptance of the Doones gave utter conviction to his writing about them. While the book was in progress he revisited Devon and Somerset. Porlock, Charles Rectory, Oare and Withypool . . . were among the places in which he refreshed his memory, tirelessly interviewing Exmoor folk and 'putting it all down in a notebook'.

Burton devotes most of his Microstudy to comparing excerpts from the text of *Lorna Doone* with the actual places (illustrated with photographs) on which Blackmore based the various episodes. This is the clearest evidence of 'romancing', but it also underlines Blackmore's skill in creating character and atmosphere and in telling an enthralling story against a background of the wild, sometimes savage, scenery that he knew so well. It was this knowledge that gave the book such depth and vividness. Here is a brief example of Blackmore's narrative and descriptive power, taken from the Preface to *Tales from the Telling House,* a collection of short stories (containing one about the Doones) published in 1896. Blackmore recollects a scene from his childhood when he stayed with his grandfather, the Rev. John Blackmore, vicar of Combe Martin and Oare.

. . . I behold an old man, with a keen profile, under a parson's shovel hat, riding a tall chestnut horse up the western slope of Exmoor, followed by his little grandson upon a shaggy and stuggy pony.

In the hazy folds of the lower hills, some four or five miles behind them, may be seen the ancient Parsonage, where the lawn is a russet sponge of moss, and a stream tinkles under the dining-room floor, and the pious rook, poised on the pulpit of his nest, reads a hoarse sermon to the chimney-pots below.

Judged by today's standards, *Lorna Doone* is overlong and too full of words; but it remains a fine piece of fiction in thc Walter Scott tradition and almost, but not quite, a great novel.

Of Blackmore's other novels (fourteen in all between 1864 and 1897) and their place in Victorian literature, I refer the reader to two discerning articles: one entitled 'The Author of "Lorna Doone" ' by Malcolm Elwin, first published in *The Literary Digest* and reprinted in the *Exmoor Review* 1981; the other, 'The Market Gardener' by Mervyn Horder, first published in the *London Magazine* and due to be reprinted in the *Exmoor Review* 1988. Two of the novels—*Clara Vaughn* and *Lorna Doone* apart—have local settings or allusions. Of *The Maid of Sker* (1873), Elwin wrote:

Like *Lorna Doone,* this novel is an autobiographical narrative in an historical setting; the hero is modelled on Girt Jan Ridd, the heroine on the demure and winsome Lorna, and Parson Chowne is a villain as ruthless and formidable as Carver Doone. Drawn with genuine genius, Chowne was based on the character of the Rev. John Froude, who kept at his Devonshire rectory during Blackmore's boyhood, not only his own pack of hounds, but a gang of vagabonds to terrorise the victims of his spleen.

Perlycross (1894) is likewise set in the Devonshire countryside of Blackmore's youth and includes a portrait of his father and other figures in the hierarchy of the self-contained village society that he grew up in. Finally in the article by Cicely Cooper, already mentioned, there is a useful brief summary of the plot of each of Blackmore's novels.

After the death of his wife in 1888, Blackmore was looked after by two nieces who continued to live in Gomer House after his own death in 1900. The house and contents were sold in 1938 to make way for a building estate, the roads around now bearing such names as Blackmore Grove, Doone Close, and Gomer Gardens. In the West Country Blackmore is commemorated by an inscribed relief portrait in Exeter Cathedral, and a copy was placed in Oare Church in 1928. By Badgworthy Water, on the way up to the Doone Valley, a large memorial stone records the 1969 centenary of the publication of *Lorna Doone*.

Hope Bourne

HOPE LILLIAN BOURNE

I first met Hope nearly thirty years ago, shortly after John Coleman-Cooke had founded the Exmoor Society and John Goodland had edited and produced the first number of the *Exmoor Review*. Hope drew the picture of Exmoor ponies for the cover of the second number published in the summer of 1960. We all used to meet in committee in those early days at Simonsbath Lodge, John Coleman-Cooke's home and the old centre of the Knight family estate. Hope came along and immediately impressed me. Here was an educated and talented woman who, through force of circumstances, had identified herself, physically and spiritually, with the Moor by living as simply as she could. By growing her own food, gathering wood for fuel, shooting for the pot, and in a variety of other ways, she was following a way of life that almost attained self-sufficiency. To pay for necessities that had to be bought, she earned a small cash income (as little as £100 p.a. in the 1950s and 1960s, saving half of it, she said) from helping out on friends' farms at sheep shearing, and tending stock; but most importantly, having taught herself to write, paint and draw, from selling the products of her pen and brush.

Such has been the pattern of her existence since coming to Exmoor after the war, but it was not her first foray into the West Country. She has vivid childhood memories of Hartland on the North Devon coast, where her mother was headmistress of the outlying village school of Elmscott. Hope loved Hartland 'with its great sea-cliffs above the ocean, and its wild hinterland like a backbone running down into Cornwall—-it greatly influenced my early life'. As Hope grew older, she became restless, 'by nature ambitious, full of energy and imagination, interested in almost everything'. She longed to make her mark. 'I felt the urge to be a great speaker, able to influence people and events, and be one of those people who make history'. But fate was less than kind. She left school at 14, and as the only daughter of a widowed mother, and afflicted with asthma, she was expected to stay at home—and she did. By the time has mother died, Hope was over 30 and faced with a crisis. All income stopped after the day of death, and the house had to be sold to pay off liabilities. With the few hundreds left over, without a home or regular income, and no profession, she decided to stand on her own feet, learn a craft, and be beholden to no-one. That decision and a twist of fate brought her down to the Somerset side of Exmoor, where her homes have been a succession of small primitive cottages or old caravans—whatever she could get—mostly in and around Withypool. For the last seventeen years she has lived in a caravan stationed at Ferny Ball, a deserted farmstead, off the track to Sherdon under Horsen Hill. This is a very remote spot, reached at best by Land Rover but normally by footslogging the last half-mile in gumboots.

In return for the use of the caravan site, a patch for growing her vegetables, and a corner of the barn for her bantams, she does various jobs for her landlord and neighbour, e.g. keeping an eye on stock and, in an emergency, digging ewes out of snowdrifts, and helping deliver lambs and calves born on the Moor. She is also licensed to shoot 'vermin' with her 12-bore shotgun and a .22 American rifle (plus telescopic sight), which means that she can shoot pigeons, rabbits, occasionally a hare, all a vital source of food for her. 'I can't be a vegetarian. Some people can but I don't feel right when I go without meat. Killing is part of Nature's pattern. He that would live with Nature must accept that law'. So armed, literally and metaphorically, she has the free run of hundreds of acres of farm land, and nobody objects.

One of the best descriptions—and appreciations—of Hope and her mode of life was written by Daniel Farson, who interviewed her in 1979 for an illustrated feature in the *Sunday Telegraph Magazine*. He was also involved in one of the two television documentaries made about her, which received national coverage. When talking to Dan, she threw light on her philosophy with remarks such as these:

> I've never taken a penny from public money. Friends tell me I could live better on National Assistance, or whatever they call it now. Over my dead body! Anyway, I've never been able to afford the stamps. I've told them this would be *more* than my entire income!
>
> It's a good life, but it's a tough life. You've got to be 100 per cent physically fit to live as I do. You've got to be tough, body and soul. Whatever happens at Ferny Ball, I've got to cope with it alone.

Her absolute dependance on good health is both a strength and a worry. She is small and robust, albeit worn by constant exposure to weather and advancing years. Hope must be in her late sixties now but, having lost her birth certificate, she simply does not know her exact age. As no-one can stop getting older, the future has its uncertainties.

As for Exmoor, she is anxious for its solitude and wildness, and about the invasion of visitors who come to explore the National Park every summer, congregating in 'honey pots' such as Tarr Steps, Malmsmead, Webber's Post, and Landacre Bridge. The fact is, of course, that but for the National Park Authority which protects the moorland from ploughing and fencing by means of management agreements, and exercises other controls for the benefit of visitors, tourism would run riot. Ironically Hope has herself contributed to the exposure of the Moor, through her work as a writer and artist.

She has written three books. *Living on Exmoor* (Galley Press, 1963) takes the form of a month-by-month diary of her activities, the shifts of the weather, the calendar of farm work, the rivers, the hills, the ancient barrows, and the wilderness around her. Each chapter is headed by a pen-and-ink drawing, supplemented by tailpieces, all most delicately done. In my opinion this is her best book, and it takes a high place in the considerable literature of Exmoor. Her next title, *A Little History of Exmoor* (Dent, 1968), explains itself—a popular account from prehistoric times, on through the chronicle of the Royal Forest, the gradual colonisation of the Moor, and the huge enterprise of John and Frederic Knight when they attempted to tame and reclaim a large part of the moorland round Simonsbath in the 19th century. This leads on to the 20th century and the designation of the National Park; but here her grasp of the narrative falters, mainly because private pressures interrupted the conclusion of her work. Her third book, *Wild Harvest* (Aycliffe Press, 1978) is a return to the personal type of commentary as in her first book—a collection of day-to-day experiences on and off farms, encounters with neighbours, local lore, and vivid descriptions of the seasons, enhanced throughout by lively drawings. She has a naturally fluent style.

As a journalist, Hope has also made her mark, notably by writing a 1,000-word column, entitled 'On Exmoor', published weekly in the *West Somerset Free Press* over a period of several years. She wrote the copy by hand in pencil and posted it to Williton every Friday, when she walked 3½ miles each way to Withypool, to collect her post and purchase necessities, packed into a rucksack for the return journey. The editor of the *Free Press* told me that the column was remarkably popular, generated a vigorous correspondence, and had a noticeable effect on circulation. Finally Hope has contributed about a dozen articles and several drawings to the *Exmoor Review*. Some of her best work is expressed in her knowledge of Exmoor farms, their history and the origins of their names. With this in mind, I recommend particularly two articles: *Tne Ancient Farms of Exmoor* (1963) and *The Hill-Farms of Exmoor* (1975).

Hope's pictures of Exmoor—a large collection of watercolours and drawings, other than those that have appeared in her books and articles—constitute an important record of her life on the Moor which, however viewed, is an extraordinary achievement. She will be remembered for her talents as author and artist, for her determined independence, yes—for her eccentricities, but above all for having had the courage to settle and survive in the wild.

Jack Hurley

JOHN EDWIN HURLEY

Jack Hurley was born and brought up in Williton, won a scholarship at Huish's Grammar School, Taunton, and then became the 'first ever' junior reporter on the *West Somerset Free Press* in August 1930 at a wage of 8 shillings a week. He went about his business on a bicycle 'with acetylene gas lamp fed from a tin of smelly carbide'. He stayed on the staff for over fifty years, chief reporter, news editor, and finally editor, a remarkable record of service to local journalism for which he was awarded the MBE in the Queen's Birthday Honours in June 1981.

Writing in the *Exmoor Review 1981,* Jack recalled the pace and pattern of village life in West Somerset in the 1930s, in many respects little different to what it had been fifty years earlier.

> The village tailors, sitting cross-legged on their kitchen tables, would make you a good suit for less than £3. A good roast dinner and a cold supper could be had off a ninepenny rabbit, and the butcher would deliver a round of beef for Sunday dinner for half-a-crown. The village barber shaved your bristles for twopence and sheared your locks for fourpence. The aroma of new-bake arose from the bread-cart, and the milkman pulled up at your door with his pony and float and dipped his measures into his pail to serve you.
>
> Many parish councils and assemblies were held in schoolrooms lit only by an oil-lamp, and it became part of my education as a young reporter to identify voices and associate them with bodies which were little more than dark shapes.

As to roads and transport—

> Many by-roads were untarred, and some villages had but recently retired their old watering carts which had sprinkled the dusty roads in summertime. Hilariously, the watering cart at Porlock had been making national news by sprinkling one side only of the high street, because the other side was in the parish of Luccombe. The private car was only for the few. The railways skirting Exmoor were busy with short distance passengers and freight, and encountering increasing competition from several bus companies. Ah! those coaches or 'charries'. Open to the sky, rattle-traps on bumpy roads, they bore us to moderately distant places on Saturday outings—happy village occasions of a sociability the private car has destroyed.

As for his job—

> The craft of the country journalist was in faithful recording of day-to-day life rather than in vivid article writing. Exmoor fifty years ago was unlikely to take up an inch of newspaper space with controversy. No amenity v. ploughing issue then. The strengths of village life were seen in social enterprises entirely local in character. Entertainment remained home-made. Village football and cricket thrived. In a few villages the friendly or benefit societies founded in the 19th century survived. Timberscombe provided a notable example. Kindness and sympathy were sterling qualities in a close-knit community. One ancient custom, that of financially helping a villager who had lost his pig (a real calamity) had not yet died out. I also remember a man going round with a notebook and inviting subscriptions to enable him to pay the bill for his wife's funeral! Village folk were so close-knit that sorrow was felt beyond the confines of the family. I recall the sound of the 'passing bell' signifying the death of a parishioner. Tolled once at intervals of a minute, it was a custom no bereaved family would break. Many times did I write, 'The blinds of houses and shops along the route of the funeral cortege were drawn as a mark of respect'.

But even funerals had their comic side—

I remember waiting at church for the arrival of a funeral party and wondering why it was so late. The answer was that the horse-drawn hearse and a motor bus had been in collision. And why? The bus had swerved because the driver had respectfully tried to lift his hat to the hearse. An incident hardly likely to occur today!

After army service, Jack returned to his old job, and it was not long afterwards that I got to know him through the Exmoor Society, an unpopular body in those days as the whole idea of conserving moorland was disliked by the majority of Exmoor farmers; and we had some in-fighting in the Society too, always good copy; but Jack invariably played fair and published balanced accounts of our aims and activities. My connection with him was, however, enormously strengthened by the five Microstudies that he wrote for the Exmoor Press, my publishing firm. These were *Murder and Mystery on Exmoor* (still our best-seller, with over 13,000 copies sold), *Snow and Storm on Exmoor, Legends of Exmoor, Exmoor in Wartime,* and *Rattle his Bones.* In each of these books, Jack deployed his encyclopedic knowledge of the region, and they form a permanent record of many aspects of the local life of West Somerset. *Rattle,* however, stood out from the others because it provided Jack with space for original research into the history of the Poor Law, with particular application to the two Exmoor workhouses of Dulverton and Williton. It was praised in all the regional papers and received national notice in the *Guardian,* which said that it 'gains enormously by concentrating on the tangible and human within a small local focus. It will chill any caring heart'.

In 1963 Jack succeeded Herbert Kille as writer of *Notes By The Way,* the weekly column of chat and miscellaneous information of essentially country interest in the *Free Press* that was to reach its centenary in April 1981. Jack then had an inspiration.

In taking up the succession I thought I would aim for a weekly yarn, put into the mouth of a mythical character. So in January 1963 the first of nearly 1,000 'Will Widden Says' appeared under that title.

So Will Widden was born and a variety of associated characters, such as Arnie Bladderwick, all of them—Jack declared—'composites of every grand old country character' he had ever met. The response was staggering; that was pleasing, but more important was the fact that Will Widden and his mates gave Jack the chance to air his deep knowledge of local accents and dialect, not just as objects of curiosity and fun but, *through* humour, to record the relics of the ancient Anglo-Saxon speech of West Somerset, with all its nuances of meaning, variety of expression, and vivid abbreviated grammar and syntax. A kind of 'verbal shorthand', Jack called it. Nothing derogatory about that. He wrote a whole article on the subject in the *Exmoor Review 1982,* and it is well worth reference and re-reading. 'Cassen go?' is one of my favourite examples of Exmoor dialect—'Owsvinum?' is another—work them out for yourself!

Williton Workhouse as described in *Rattle his Bones* *Hole*

Jack was a man of many interests. He was a football fan and often attended the Wembley Cup Final in the days when tickets were relatively easy to come by. He was fond of acting, worked with the blind playwright, Phoebe Rees, who wrote *The White Dove of Bardon;* and he was a member of the Nettlecombe Players when they won the Sybil Thorndike Trophy. But his major passion was for music. He was an accomplished organist, played the organ at Williton Methodist Church for over fifty years, or on more than 5,000 Sundays. And, while reckoning up statistics, he once said that, by the time he retired as editor of the *Free Press*, he had written more than 20 million words. He died in 1983.

Richard Jefferies W. *Strang*

JOHN RICHARD JEFFERIES

Richard Jefferies was the son of a small farmer, born in 1848 at Coate on the edge of Swindon, and grew up in what was then a separate village. He went to school in Swindon as a day boy and supplemented his education, partly by reading, but more practically by wandering around the countryside of the White Horse, watching wild life, farming (though no farmer himself), and the changing seasons. By looking and listening he absorbed a vast amount of information and grew up into an accomplished naturalist. At the age of 17 he became a reporter on a local newspaper and learned his trade the hard way, as Jack Hurley did on the *Free Press* at Williton.

In the spring of 1872 Joseph Arch founded the National Agricultural Labourers' Union, whose object was 'to raise wages' (then standing at 12s a week or less), 'shorten hours, and make a man out of a land-tied slave'. The Union attracted members from all over the Midlands and South and West; strikes broke out; and society was amazed at this 'rural uprising'. In November Jefferies made history by writing three letters to *The Times* concerning 'The Wiltshire Labourer', a factual and forceful statement of the lives and working conditions of the farm workers in his county. These letters created a sensation for they told the public the plain truth; and so, in one bound, at the age of 24, Richard Jefferies became a household name.

Within a few years he had set up as a freelance writer, an expert on rural subjects, contributing frequently to a wide range of periodicals including the *Fortnightly, Pall Mall Gazette, Manchester Guardian,* and a variety of farm and livestock journals. A number of these articles were collected into volumes and published under titles such as *The Gamekeeper at Home* (1878), *Wild Life in a Southern County* (1879), *Round about a Great Estate* (1880), *The Life of the Fields* (1884), and *Field and Hedgerow* (1889), a posthumous publication. He also wrote a number of separate books. Apart from some inferior novels, there was *Amaryllis at the Fair,* a charming story based on family life at Coate; *After London,* a fantasy woven round the idea of what might happen after a natural catastrophe had flooded the south of England and the countryside had reverted to jungle; *Bevis,* a boy's book of adventures constructed out of childhood memories of Coate Reservoir; and *The Story of My Heart,* a long poetic reflection upon Nature, regarded by some as his greatest work.

Jefferies died of chronic fibroid phthisis in 1887 after years of torturing illness. He was extraordinarily prolific, twenty-three books in a short life of 38 years, and for that reason the quality of his writing is often uneven. In other words he wrote too much and too quickly—he had to, in order to make ends meet—but, at his best, he was able to transmit his acute observations and comments upon the life around him in lucid, lyrical, at times mystical, language, which was inspired.

I have left until now mention of Jefferies' connection with Exmoor. It is to be found in one book, *Red Deer* (1884), and in three essays—'The Water-Colley' and 'By the Exe' (both included in *The Life of the Fields),* and 'Summer in Somerset' (included in *Field and Hedgerow).* To take the essays first. 'The Water-Colley' was first published in the *Manchester Guardian* of 31 August 1883. C. P. Scott, the editor, was one of Jefferies' most stalwart friends, helped raise funds to support him in his last illness and prevailed on him to accept a grant of £100 from The Royal Literary Fund, an offer that Jefferies had rejected earlier with contempt. In this essay he relates that 'the sweet grass was wet with dew as I walked through a meadow in Somerset to the river'—probably the Exe. He watches the bumble-bees, butterflies and moths; hears the corncrake so adept at concealment; picks an orchid in a meadow tinted pink by its profusion; and fishes leisurely for trout. Then he sees the water-colley or dipper, 'like a starling with a white neck'.

> I did not see him till he was on the wing. Away he flew with a call like a young bird just tumbled out of its nest, following the curves of the stream. Presently I saw him through an alder bush which hid me; he was perched on a root of alder under the opposite bank.
>
> He bobbed himself up and down as he perched on the root in the oddest manner, bending his legs so that his body almost touched his perch, and rising again quickly, this repeated in quick succession as if curtsying. This motion with him is a sign of uncertainty—it shows suspicion; after he had bobbed to me ten times, off he went.
>
> Upon a ledge of rock I saw him once more, but there was no hedge to hide me, and he would not feed . . . Calling in an injured tone, as if much annoyed, he flew, swept round the meadow, and so to the river behind me. His friend followed . . . Some accuse them of taking the ova of trout, and they are shot at trout nurseries; but it is doubtful if they are really guilty . . . It is the birds and other creatures peculiar to the water that render fly-fishing so pleasant; were they all destroyed, and nothing left but the mere fish, one might as well stand and fish in a stone cattle-trough.

'By the Exe' was first published in *The Standard* of 26 September 1883. About half of it is devoted to the otter, then still numerous and regularly hunted. Jefferies describes its physique in detail—'the great width of the upper nostril', 'the length and sharpness of the hold-fast teeth', and 'the sturdiness and roundness of the chest or barrel, expressive of singular strength'; and adds that its short legs are an addition to its strength, 'which is perhaps greater than that of any other animal of proportionate size', and that 'he weighs nearly as heavy as a fox'. Then follows a closely worded account of a chase and kill, told without comment in a factual dispassionate manner that would probably offend most readers today. Towards the end of the essay, however, he puts in a plea for preservation, especially in rivers like the Thames, 'where he is treated as a venomous cobra might be on land'.

The truth is the otter is a most interesting animal and worth preservation, even at the cost of what he eats. There is a great difference between keeping the number of otters down by otter-hunting within reasonable limits and utterly exterminating them. Hunting the otter in Somerset is one thing, exterminating them in the Thames another.

Were he alive today, Jefferies would be sad to learn that the otter has now disappeared from Exmoor.

'Summer in Somerset' was first published in *The English Illustrated Magazine* in 1887 and illustrated by John William North, Jefferies' artist friend, who had settled in West Somerset and, after marriage, lived for ten years (1884-1894) at Beggearn Huish House, north of Roadwater. Before that, North had lodged with a Mrs. Thorne and her son first at Halsway, Crowcombe, and then at Woolston Moor Farm (now known as Woolston Grange). It was at Woolston, it is thought, that Jefferies came to stay in the early summer of 1883 to write the three essays already mentioned, and to research for the composition of *Red Deer,* published in the following year, and of which 'Summer in Somerset' was a by-product. It did not appear in print until the year of his death.

In this third essay Jefferies devotes the first four pages to a close but lyrical description of the Barle, from its source down to Tarr Steps (Torre, he spells it). And then:

In a cottage some way up the hill we ate clotted cream and whortleberry jam. Through the open door came the ceaseless rush! rush! like a wind in the wood. The floor was of concrete, lime and sand; on the open hearth—pronounced "airth"—sods of turf cut from the moor and oak branches were smouldering under the chimney crook. Turf smoke from the piled-up fires of winter had darkened the beams of the ceiling, but from that rude room there was a view of the river, and the hill, and the oaks in full June colour, which the rich would envy. Sometimes in early morning the wild red deer are seen feeding on the slope opposite.

By a mossy bank a little girl—a miniature Audrey—stout, rosy and ragged, stood with a yellow straw hat aslant on her yellow hair, eating the leaves from a spray of beech in her hand. Audrey looked at us, eating the beech leaves steadily, but would not answer, not even "Where's your father to?" . . . but when a penny was put in her hand she began to move, and made off for home with her treasure.

Entering Dulverton, he found the road 'jammed tight between cottages':

. . . so narrow is the lane that foot passengers huddle up in doorways to avoid the touch of the wheels, and the windows of the houses are protected by iron bars like cages lest the splash-boards should crack the glass . . . The farm labourers, filing homewards after their day's work, each carries poles of oak or faggots on their shoulders for their hearths, generally oak branches; it is their perquisite.

And so Jefferies and North found their way back—by pony trap, most likely—to Woolston and the Quantocks with their 'thumb-nail ridges', and to a sight of Flatholm and Steepholm that seemed to lie 'float in the dim sea'.

The day goes over like a white cloud; as the sun declines it is pleasant to go into the orchard—the vineyard of Somerset, and then perhaps westward may be seen a light in the sky by the horizon as if thrown up from an immense mirror under. The mirror is the Severn Sea . . .

In her article, 'Richard Jefferies' Exmoor Summer', printed in the *Exmoor Review 1987,* Berta Lawrence reminds us of how Jefferies delighted in the legends and customs of the country, such as wassailling, the local speech, and the old-fashioned farm practices still extant—for example, the use of the sickle for reaping and how the reaper sharpened the blade by drawing it through an apple. Of a walk up through the woods at Selworthy, to Holnicote House, and the prevalence of thatch on the Acland estate, he writes:

Thrushes sang, and chaffinches, and sweetest of all, if simplest in notes, the greenfinches talked and courted in the trees . . . There was a sense of rest and quiet, and with it a joyousness of bird-life, such as should be about an English homestead.

Red Deer was Jefferies' only full-length book about Exmoor. He wrote it with the help of the Heal family of Exford, with whom—almost certainly—he stayed during June 1883, after leaving Woolston. Fresh light has been thrown on this episode by Arthur C. Clarke, the world-famous science fiction writer, in an article published by *The Field* in May 1948, the centenary of Jefferies' birth. Arthur Clarke is the great-grandson of Arthur Heal, Huntsman of the Devon and Somerset Staghounds 1871-1889, a man of great reputation in hunting circles, and who had joined the 'D and S' as whipper-in (to Jack Babbage) in 1855—the year when Fenwick Bisset, a man no less highly regarded, became Master and who saved the deer from extinction by poaching, and then revived both the population of the deer and the popularity of deer hunting.

In addition to his duties as Huntsman, Arthur Heal farmed at North Ley, near the Kennels at Exford, and he must have been a fruitful source of information. But it was Fred Heal, Arthur's bachelor son, who lived with his parents, a hunting man, who had three farms of his own—and thus a true man of the moor—who conducted Jefferies over Exmoor and taught him about the deer. These facts were revealed to Arthur Clarke, when a worn copy of *Red Deer* came into his hands and found 'to be sheltering a number of of letters from Jefferies'. I quote:

The book bears the inscription: "Fred. G. Heal, Esq. From the Author, Jan. 10th, 1884", and it is amusing to read in the introduction to the Constable edition of *The Story of My Heart* that when Jefferies had requested some more copies of this book Longman replies testily that he had already had sixteen and could not his friends buy them? This must have been one of the volumes whose generous distribution had aroused the publisher's protests.

These letters probably form part of a more extensive series, and though they are largely concerned with stag-hunting they throw a considerable light on Jefferies' personality and show that his long fight against ill-health had destroyed neither his kindliness nor his range of interests.

Arthur Heal, Huntsman of the Devon and Somerset Staghounds, 1871-1889 *How*

Since, as Arthur Clarke said, the letters were largely concerned with queries about the deer, I do not propose to quote from them here: except to say that Jefferies sent Fred Heal a presentation copy of the book on 10 January 1884, and wrote to him for the last time on 16 September of that year. By that time his health had irretrievably broken down.

In *Red Deer* Jefferies clothed the facts supplied by Fred and Arthur Heal, and his own observations, in his customary lucid style. The result is a fine and readable record of the life cycle and habits of the deer, and of the methods and pattern of hunting; but it also revealed an Exmoor that, in many respects, no longer exists. Early on in the book he refers to

> . . . the smooth outline of the moors, without a fence for miles together . . . Heather covers the largest part of the ground, which is never ploughed or sown, and where there are no flower-grown meads . . . The plough has not touched it, and civilisation has not come near.

But not everything is unfamiliar or primeval.

> A long winter of eight months, with continuous rains and heavy fogs, is succeeded by a hot, short summer. When the sun shines, the fierce rays pour down on the heather and dry it till it is hard and wiry . . . Innumerable bees gather to the heather-bells; it is a question where they all come from; they must travel long distances to the feast of honey.
>
> The whortleberries ripen, and women and children go out to pick them. It is their harvest of the year; tons and tons—whole truck-loads—are sent away by railroad.

That has happened within living memory. People still pick 'urts, but for themselves only, and the railroad is not what it was. Jefferies briefly mentions the large-scale reclamation carried out by John and Frederic Knight of Simonsbath, and in a faintly disparaging tone—possibly the Heals disapproved—but adds:

> The farmhouses are now occupied by Scotch shepherds. If you knock at the door a Scotch face appears, and you are offered a glass of milk, to which you are "varra" welcome. The boundless heather, the deep glens, and the red deer correspond to the Gaelic accent.

That was John Gourdie—or his wife—who had brought down one of the last consignments of Cheviot sheep to Exmoor, and who rented Wintershead from 1898 until his death in 1931. Exford was 'absolutely isolated . . . ten miles to the nearest station and there is no telegraph'.

> The hamlet street is level for a little distance, but with this exception no-one can move from his doorstep without going uphill, unless it be to wade along the river . . . Some considerable part of the first two miles on the slopes above the Exe is cultivated . . . One owner encloses a piece one year, another the next; and thus Exmoor is nibbled at. The circle slowly spreads, but so slowly as to make no apparent impression; some fields, too, have fallen back to rushes.

Little if anything escapes Jefferies. He describes the system and effects of swaling; notices the boggy areas signalled by tufts of cotton grass; and spots the stacks of turf, cut and drying for winter fuel—the ashes having 'an agricultural value for drilling in with turnips'. He remarks on the wide-ranging habits of the deer that roam within a triangle of territory bounded by a line drawn from Bridgwater to Ilfracombe to Exeter and back to Bridgwater again. The hedges, he says, mostly of beech, growing on top of banks of loose stones and earth, are 'ten feet high, and as much through'. Out of them droop long grass and moss 'like arras', also ferns and, in the crevices, hart's-tongue. Jefferies' narrative, as he wanders over the moor, flows like running water; but his chief aim is to watch the deer.

Six out of the ten chapters in the book are devoted to a close account of the deer, their habits, and the art of the chase. These chapters have to be read in full to appreciate their intimate knowledge and lyrical expression. I refer briefly to the description of Cloutsham Ball, 'a skull-cap of green velvet imitated in sward'; of a sudden sight of a stag standing 'breast-deep in the brake'; of Horner Mill with its large iron overshot wheel—

> Once a hind closely followed was so beset by the hounds that, unable to quit the brook, she leaped from the sluice on to the top of the revolving wheel. The immense iron wheel carried her over and threw her to the ground, disabling her. She was immediately killed to prevent suffering.

One short chapter is devoted to Combe Sydenham, deep in the valley near Monksilver, hoary in history and legend; but this is by way of an appendix, included possibly because the manor house was easy to visit from Woolston. *Red Deer* is about the red deer of Exmoor, and it remains one of the very best accounts in the literature of natural history.

ANNIE BERTA LAWRENCE

Berta Lawrence is a Somerset writer, in my view insufficiently appreciated for the depth of her knowledge of local life and history, or for the elegance and fluency of her writing, whether prose or verse. Her output is not large, but by working within the relatively narrow confines of her subjects, she represents—for me and for others who know her work—the best kind of regional writer. How has this come about?

Like others who have been attracted to the south-west and repaid that attraction by contributing to the cultural character of the area, Berta came from 'up country'. Born and brought up in Buckinghamshire, she studied English and French for a London University degree and gained First Class Honours. She then obtained a Diploma in Education at Reading University, and left England to lecture in English Language and Literature at the University of Clermont Ferrand in France. She also taught English in three French schools. It was in France before the war that she met her future husband, John F. Lawrence. Together they moved to Bridgwater where he became a

John and Berta Lawrence

teacher of history at Dr. Morgan's Grammar School for Boys and later Deputy Head. At times Berta also taught French at the Girls' Grammar School, as well as English at the French Convent in Langport. They have made Bridgwater their home ever since.

When her two children were young, Berta started writing children's stories and verses, contributing to *Child Education* for over twenty years, also to BBC Children's Hour radio programmes. This was the prelude to active freelancing, writing short stories, some for radio, others for magazines such as *Chambers' Journal* and *Good Housekeeping*, besides a variety of articles on literary, topographical and historical subjects for *The Lady, Guardian, The Countryman, Western Morning News, South West Catholic History, Somerset and West,* and *Dorset Life*; likewise for the journals of the Charles Lamb Society and the Thomas Hardy Society. Between 1967 and 1987 she contributed no less than twelve poems and as many articles to the *Exmoor Review,* and thus became one of its most prolific and regular authors. She has written eight books, including two novels, *The Bond of Green Withy* (1954), a Country Book Club Choice, and *The Nightingale in the Branches* (1955), both published by Werner Laurie; also two books about the Quantocks—*Quantock Country* (Westaway 1952) and *Discovering the Quantocks* (Shire 1974). For the publishers, David & Charles, she wrote two titles, both self-explanatory, *Coleridge and Wordsworth in Somerset* (1970) and *Somerset Legends* (1973). Finally, there are her first book, *A Somerset Journal* (Westaway 1951), and her last, *Exmoor Villages* (Exmoor Press 1984). Her husband is co-author with John Hamilton of *Men and Mining in the Quantocks* (Town and Country Press 1970).

Exmoor finds its way, as of right, into *A Somerset Journal*. By working forward through the year from January to December, Berta records the literary and historical associations, customs and personalities, present or past, as they have occurred or when she discovered them—a neat device that lends interest to every month and yields a rich crop of people and events. The Exmoor examples include wassailling at Carhampton (January), Cleeve Abbey (March), the Brendon Hills and Crowcombe (May), sheepskin dressing at Old Cleeve (June), and Walter Raymond, another Somerset writer, at Withypool (October). These passages form part of a highly informative itinerary, delightfully described and abounding in items of interest, some of which were already disappearing when the book was published in 1951. For example, the teazle harvest at Thornfalcon; or the Quantock broom squire who apologised for having to charge two shillings for one of his beautiful brooms made of birch twigs or heather, with oak or ash handles. *A Somerset Journal* is a jewel of a book that deserves re-printing, just as it stands.

The *Exmoor Villages* Microstudy bears a certain resemblance to the *Journal* in that Berta describes some sixty places in the National Park in terms of their background of wild life and their historical and literary associations. As her publisher, I find it hard to be impartial; even so, having declared my interest, I can confidently assert my admiration for the way in which she writes 500 words or so about a village such as Monksilver, or the coastal hamlet of Porlock Weir, or—in about 1200 words—deals deftly with the riches of Dunster. A remarkable achievement when viewed as a work of 'vivid condensation', handy for the kind of visitor who is willing to read something more than a handful of captions and capable of appreciating good English.

It is however in the *Exmoor Review,* where she has more room to manoeuvre, that one finds perhaps some of her best writing. The Brendons are obviously a favourite subject, and there are articles about them in three of the issues. In Volume 21 (1980), in *Quaker Farmer in the Brendons,* Berta tells the story of the settlement and sufferings of William Lyddon and his wife Elizabeth, a Dulverton girl, at Swansea

Farm in the parish of Withiel Florey. It is a compelling tale, as powerful as a Bronte novel, and told with the force that the subject deserves— of Elizabeth, bearing and rearing nine children, running a farmhouse in wild isolated country, supervising the husbandry of their rough acres and the care of their flocks, while William is condemned to spend a total of fifteen years in Ilchester Gaol, 'a vile and notorious place', for his faith. Parallels in present-day Soviet Russia spring to mind. In contrast is her article in Volume 24 (1983) about John William North, the painter, who came to West Somerset in 1868 and spent over fifty years there, living successively at Halsway Manor, Woolston Moor Farm, Beggearn Huish House, Bilbrook, Withycombe, and finally Leighland. He was a friend of Richard Jefferies (the centenary of whose birth Berta celebrated in the 1987 *Review*), and put him up when he visited Exmoor in 1883 to write *Red Deer*. North also helped raise funds for Jefferies' impoverished widow. His pictures of Exmoor, rather sweet and sentimental, but sensitive in the style of Birket Foster took the countryside of Exmoor and West Somerset into galleries at home and abroad. One of Exford, and another of the river Barle, are reproduced in the 1983 *Review*.

Over the years Berta has contributed articles to the *Review* on Walter Raymond; Walter Wilkinson, the travelling puppeteer and his novelist wife, Winifred; Dom Philip Powel, the Roman Catholic priest sheltered in the early 17th century by the Poyntz family at Leigh Barton; Robert Southey at the Ship Inn, Porlock, where he consumed laver-bread, a local speciality made from edible seaweed; and a moving tribute to Maureen Hosegood, the poet, also connected with Leigh Barton, who died at Hillfarrance, near Taunton, at the early age of 46. Maureen had a lyrical gift expressed with delicacy and discipline in a handful of poems, some of which have appeared in the *Review*. It is these same qualities that characterise Berta's own poems, a dozen of which have been published in the *Review* over the past ten years, as noted earlier. As an example of her work at its best, and of particular application to Exmoor since it is written about Clicket, the small abandoned settlement in the Brendons; here is:

DESERTED VILLAGE

Dead now, old people who remembered
Grandparents from Clicket.

Clicket too is dead, like a corner of Roman Gaul
Buried in a valley cupped by Brendon Hills.
You can excavate it, find stones of a linhay-wall
Or a fragment of byre-pillar from a farm
Called Thorn or Combe;
Find a mill-stone cast under dead branches
Near the leat choked with many years' leaves,
Or a bit of leaded window from a cottage.

Discover Clicket among gorse-thickets and broom,
Among wilding fruit trees, Combe's orchard once,
Under rich layers of leaf-mould
Beneath walnut-trees rifled by boys
Long after Clicket grew silent.

Silent, except for the note of the stream
(They say there are trout there still)
Birdsong from a copse tangled with flowers,
Rustle of rabbit or stoat in the bracken,
Bark of the fox after dark
And moan of the wind through a roofless mill.

In a year when farmers and politicians argue about food surpluses and the need to take three million acres out of farming, shall we see more Clickets, one day, on Exmoor?

PHOEBE MEIRION REES

Miss Rees was born at Martock in East Somerset in the year 1900. Her father, Harry, was a parson, later vicar of Chipstable, high up in the Brendon Hills, where the Capel family had been squires for generations at Bulland Lodge. Phoebe had been christened after *H.M.S. Phoebe* which, under the command of her great-grandfather, Captain Hillyer (later Admiral Sir James), defeated the American man-of-war, *Essex*, in a battle in the war of 1812. As a child Phoebe shared a governess with the Capels, enjoyed country pursuits and watched the deer in the woods. She was sent to school at St. Anne's, Abbots Bromley near Stafford (the home of the Horn Dance performed annually in September) rose to be head girl, and was then accepted for a place at Newnham College, Cambridge. As it turned out—in order to be near her Aunt Gertrude who was seriously ill and living in the Midlands—she became a student at Birmingham University and graduated there. This change was not without its compensations, for it brought her into contact with the renowned Birmingham Repertory Theatre, founded and directed by Barry Jackson, an experience that instilled in her a passion for drama.

After university, Phoebe turned down a job on the *Birmingham Post*, and came south to London to teach history and English at Queen's College, Harley Street, where she remained two years. In 1928 however she responded once more to an appeal to look after her aunt, whose husband, the Rev. Fred Corfield, had become rector of Nettlecombe, a scattered parish, a few miles south-east of Washford, within the present borders of the National Park. It was there that she became a close friend of the Trevelyan family, then in residence at Nettlecombe Court

Phoebe Rees *Jane Cox*

(now the Leonard Wills Field Centre), and where—first in the rectory and then, after her uncle's retirement, in a bungalow built at The Sanctuary, Five Bells, near Watchet—she decided to live for the rest of her life. Her association with West Somerset has therefore lasted over thirty years.

However, it was while she was taking care of her aunt in the 1930s that Phoebe made up her mind to revive her early love of drama, and employ her mind and energies in writing plays, suitable principally for performance by village dramatic societies and Women's Institutes: which meant *inter alia* writing a number of one-act pieces, many of them for women only, and often in dialect. Phoebe also founded the Nettlecombe players, an amateur company that won a high reputation in county and regional festivals and, in 1939, was awarded the Sybil Thorndike Trophy. This was for Phoebe's dramatisation of Thomas Hardy's *The Trumpet-Major,* in which she herself played the leading part opposite Jack Hurley, journalist, and St. John Couch, lawyer, both men of note in the district. Her first play, *That There Dog,* had appeared eight years earlier in 1931. Written originally in Somerset speech and based on a real incident reported in the *West Somerset Free Press,* it was entered for the village drama festival organised by the Somerset Rural Community Council, and received such excellent reviews that it was subsequently broadcast from Bristol. A heartening start, it was the first of over fifty plays, most of them published and performed in village halls, barns, churches, and small stages all over Somerset and the south-west, and some in English-speaking countries abroad—a remarkable achievement that earned Phoebe the award of the O.B.E.

Two of Phoebe's plays, whose themes are closely associated with Exmoor. have taken wing far beyond the confines of Somerset. The first of these, *The White Dove of Bardon,* a three-act play with a cast of sixteen men and women, was written originally for radio, and first broadcast in the BBC West Region programme on Boxing Day 1948. It caught the attention of Val Gielgud, head of BBC radio drama, and aroused so much interest, that it was repeated both in the Monday Night Theatre Series of the Home Service and in the Overseas Service. It was also performed in stage version, as one of thirteen three-act plays written by members of the Somerset Guild of Playwrights to tell 'The Story of Somerset'.

The theme therefore is historical and concerns Bardon, a pleasant country house of ancient origin, nowadays 18th century in outward appearance, that lies in a secluded situation in the parish of Old Cleeve. In the Middle Ages it may have had some connection with the Cistercian abbey, whose ruins lie barely a mile distant. In the late 16th century the house came into the possession of a lawyer, Robert Leigh, and remained the family home for nearly 300 years. One day in 1836 his descendant, William Leigh, was told by a servant that an attic window had been broken. He ordered its repair; but when it had been broken thrice more—not by a mischievous boy as first thought, but by a white dove seen striking repeatedly at the pane—irritation drove him to have the attic searched. In it was discovered an ancient chest, later referred to as the 'Throckmorton Box', that contained State papers concerning the relations between Queen Elizabeth I and Mary Queen of Scots, after the latter had become a virtual prisoner in England in 1568. It was a tense period of Romanist plots and Protestant vigilance in high places. The planting of spies and forgeries, and the use of torture were commonplace; and no means were spared by either side to gain mastery. Mary herself was involved, willy nilly, in a series of conspiracies, e.g. one by Francis Throckmorton who was caught and executed in 1584, and another by Anthony Babington who suffered the same fate two years later. Ultimately Mary was tried by a commission of peers, convicted, and beheaded at Fotheringay on 8 February 1587. The documents found at Bardon indicated that she had been convicted on evidence forged and planted by Francis Walsingham, head of State security; and that her protestation of innocence in any plot to assassinate Elizabeth was genuine. The dove was never seen again.

Leigh forebears were involved in these intricate intrigues which lent credence to the mystery; and there were other tales—unconnected with the papers—of a ghostly lady playing a spinet or harpsichord, and of a heavy coach crunching up the drive. Bardon has had its full share of atmospheric history! It remains to say that all the papers found in the attic were sent to the British Museum in 1870, were edited by an historian, Charles Cotton, who had married into the Leigh family, and printed in the Camden Society publications, third series, No. 7, in 1909. So much for a summary of the fascinating material, which Phoebe fashioned into her compelling play.

The second work, *The Miraculous Year,* concerns the twelve months (all but three weeks) that Dorothy Wordsworth and her brother, William, spent at Alfoxden House, near Holford, between 16 July 1797 and 26 June 1798. The play is divided into two Acts and contains seven characters, all women—Dorothy herself; Sara, wife of Samuel Taylor Coleridge, then living nearby at Nether Stowey; Mrs. Poole, mother of Tom Poole, wealthy tanner and friendly neighbour; Charlotte Poole, an unfriendly cousin of Tom; and two maid servants. The dialogue and plot is largely based on Dorothy's letters and journal, on Charlotte's diary, on reminiscences of a Poole descendant, and background knowledge. The scene is set in Tom Poole's house in Nether Stowey, and the action derives directly from the dialogue.

Although Dorothy later referred to this year as the 'annus mirabilis', hence the title of the play, in fact it was an uncomfortable time for her, her brother, and the Coleridges.

Like 1940, this was a period when England felt herself under threat of invasion, regarded Napoleon as a monster and all Frenchmen (other than royalists) as highly dangerous, and panicked at even the most liberal sentiments expressed at home, let alone those attributed to outright reformers and republicans, such as Tom Paine, author of *The Rights of Man.* Such were the sources of suspicion, added to innate native distrust of strangers, that attached to the Wordsworths and Coleridge during 1797-8. Gossip grew around their strange habits of walking about the woods and hills and along the coast at night (looking for landing places for the French?); and when they made expeditions on foot to Watchet, and to places as far afield as Dulverton, Porlock and Lynton, putting up where they could overnight. Their explanation—that the two men were seeking inspiration for poetry—was received with incredulity, to say the least. Yet this was nothing less than the truth for, although Wordsworth had barely begun to write, Coleridge was in full flood. *The Ancient Mariner,* for example, grew in his mind as he and the Wordsworths walked across the northern spur of the Quantocks on their way to Watchet and distant Lynton.

The Miraculous Year has been among the most successful and widest acclaimed of Phoebe's plays. Her achievement was the more remarkable when it is realised that she wrote it *after* she had contracted a rare disease, *sarcoidosis,* which has left her totally blind for the past thirty years. For a time too she became deaf, and she remembers with joy that moment of recovery when, suddenly, she could hear the birds. Fortunately she had completed the necessary research for the play beforehand but, on coming out of hospital, she set herself to learn touch-typing of a rough kind, supplemented by dictation on to audio tapes, made possible by the gift of a tape recorder by friends. In this manner the MS was drafted, revised and put together in its final form. Phoebe was registered as blind in November 1953, but she has coped with everyday life ever since and has continued to write plays.

The Miraculous Year has had a most unexpected sequel. Recently an order for 2000 copies of the play was received from the University of Kyoto. The text had been annotated in 1983 by Professors T. Harada and T. Sugino, is now in use as a set book for students, and may well keep its place as a classic among academics. It would be intriguing to learn how a Japanese student converts the pithy Somerset remarks of the maid servant, Hannah Dibble, into equivalent 'argo' of his own countryside.

Leslie Wedlake *R. Priddy*

ALFRED LESLIE WEDLAKE

If the name of any one man be linked with that of a single place, not as a landowner or captain of industry, but as historian and interpreter of the past, then there is no better example than that of A. L. Wedlake and the port of Watchet on the north Somerset coast, a place closely associated with Exmoor throughout its history.

Leslie Wedlake was born in Watchet in 1900 and, except for one year, has lived and worked in the town ever since. Educated at the school attached to the Methodist Chapel, he left at the age of 14 and went first as a junior to the Wansborough Paper Company, then in 1916 to the newly launched Exmoor Paper and Bag Company. In 1919 he went to London and worked for a year in a marine insurance office in Threadneedle Street, using his spare time to visit museums and bookshops in Charing Cross Road. In August 1920 he returned to Watchet as clerk of works to the Cardiff Shipbreaking Company engaged in breaking up the cruiser, *H.M.S. Fox.* Two years later he rented (and eventually acquired) 2½ acres of land from the Wyndham Estate in the Doniford Road, where he started a nursery garden and floral business, and which he conducted with the help of his son until retirement in 1982. In public life he served on the Watchet Urban District Council for twenty years, and was a member of the Court Leet for over 25 years.

Keenly interested in archaeology and local history since a youth, he was elected to the Somerset Archaeological and Natural History Society in the 1940s (he was its President in 1981-2), and about the same time joined the Prehistoric Society. He was also active as a tutor in local history for the Workers' Educational Association. A prolific academic journalist, he has contributed articles to the *Proceedings* of the S.A.N.H.S., to Somerset and Dorset *Notes and Queries,* and to the *Exmoor Review.* He has also written monographs on *The Prehistory of West Somerset, Saxon Watchet and the Mint, The History of Watchet Market House,* and *A Brief History of Watchet,* all published in the late 1970s.

His principal published work has been *A History of Watchet,* first issued by Cox of Williton in 1955, followed by a second larger edition by the Exmoor Press in 1973. Both books are now comparatively rare. The work is over 160 pages long, illustrated, and covers the whole span from early man to present times. The first chapter, which deals with geology and pre-history, is of particular interest, since this is one of the author's prime subjects. Much of the narrative is the product of his own researches, and of his discoveries of prehistoric implements in the area, beautifully drawn and reproduced in the text. The reader soon becomes aware of another of Mr. Wedlake's enthusiasms—the Saxon occupation of the West, in particular the growth of Watchet as an important port, with its own Mint. A whole page in the book is devoted to the illustration of coins struck at Watchet between the reigns of Aethelred II and Stephen, and located in museum collections by the author himself.

The story then proceeds readably and in easy stages, packed with facts and incidents, through the troubled Middle Ages; taking in the rise of the landowning families of Luttrell, Sydenham and Wyndham; the building of the local fleet of sailing ships; the constant repair of the harbour against assaults of the sea; the rise (and fall) of early industries, e.g. fishing, manufacture of cloth, mining of alabaster and gypsum, paper making (happily active today), the export of iron ore from the Brendon Hills; and the construction of turnpikes and railways. The author is no less interested in farm practice, the origins of field and place names, the history of schools, and of churches and chapels (not forgetting the literary associations of the parish church of St. Decuman, standing like a sentinel above town, so welcome to the 'Ancient Mariner'); and among much else the survival of customs, the rise of local government, and the variety of occupations and personalities that have, in their time, characterised Watchet. As Wilfred Seaby, former curator of the County Museum at Taunton, wrote in the Introduction to the book:

> Here we find a common meeting ground for practical archaeological fieldwork, enquiry into original source material, both written and oral, and a carefully balanced interpretation of the known facts.

It was thanks to Mr. Wedlake's immense store of knowledge and the unique collection of photographs and slides that he assembled throughout his life—an essential part of the process of research—that a second book followed in 1984. This was *Old Watchet, Williton and Around,* a Microstudy of 76 pages issued by the Exmoor Press, packed with pictures and a connecting text. These two books, the History and the Microstudy, not to mention the articles and monographs, would normally be sufficient to attest Mr. Wedlake's achievement as the historian of Watchet. But there is another, no less concrete piece of evidence—the Watchet Market House Museum, of which he was co-founder and inspirer (together with Ben Norman, author of *Tales of Watchet Harbour,* and several other friends). Not only has he contributed many of the early artefacts that he discovered, but his example encouraged others who live in or love Watchet to donate a whole variety of exhibits to what has now become one of the most attractive collections in the West Country. The museum was opened by George Wyndham on 14 July 1979, is staffed by volunteers, and kept open between the end of May and September. It is visited by over 13,000 people annually.

HENRY WILLIAMSON

In his article, 'Tarka in Question' (*Exmoor Review 1987*), Alan Jenkins wrote this about Henry Williamson's best-seller:

> Having read it at the age of fifteen, when it was first published in 1927, it came to me as a marvellous, almost physical experience, its seductive, detailed writing vastly different from that of other animal writers . . .

For many readers, *Tarka the Otter,* is even today the only book of consequence that Williamson ever wrote, with a possible runner-up in *Salar the Salmon.* For them, in short, Williamson was solely a Nature writer. He always resented that designation, although undoubtedly he worshipped Nature in place of the Almighty, and genuflected before Richard Jefferies as the Messiah. But, first, a few facts.

Henry Williamson was born on 1st December 1895 at Brockley on the south-east edge of London, and received a suburban upbringing, but with easy access to the open countryside of which he took full advantage. On 4 November 1914, shortly before his 19th birthday, he enlisted in the London Rifle Brigade—later he claimed that he had joined up at the age of 16½, but that was one of the numerous fantasies he turned into fact. In France he endured front line service, but came through the war physically unscathed. Mentally, not so. The incident that cut deeply into his memory, indeed it altered his whole life—and he repeated the telling of it *ad nauseam*—was the 1914 Christmas truce when, in his section of the line, British and German soldiers climbed out of their trenches to meet in in No Man's Land and fraternise, before finally firing was resumed. In one of his later and wilder fantasies, he asserted that Corporal Hitler had been among the German party.

The second seminal event occurred after demobilisation in September 1919, when he discovered a secondhand copy of Jefferies' *The Story of My Heart* at a shop in Folkestone:

> I stood there more than an hour, so rapt was I in the pages, which were a revelation to me of my own self, which had been smothered all through the hectic days of war.

He returned to civilian life 'without the least intention of doing any work for my living. except by writing'. However, after his gratuity of £100 was exhausted, he had no recourse but to find employment of a sort—first as an advertising salesman, and then as a 'motoring correspondent' in Fleet Street. But these were stop-gaps and eventually, in 1921, he left London for good and migrated down to Georgeham in North Devon which he had visited on holiday before the war. Here he rented a cottage for £5 a year, paid out of a very slender income, sustained only by intermittent freelancing. He was not poverty stricken all the time, however. Four years later, in 1925, he married Loetitia Hib-

Henry Williamson *Ossie Jones*

bert on the strength of a cheque for £500 received from the *Saturday Evening Post,* and moved into a roomier dwelling in the same village. Life nonetheless was hard, especially when the first baby arrived and Loetitia fell ill, which meant that Henry had to cope with feeds and nappies. It did not improve his temper and he felt himself to be a martyr—even so, all good copy later! By that time he had long settled down to practise what he regarded as his true *metier,* that of novelist.

It was at Georgeham that he wrote the sequence of four novels later combined into *The Flax of Dream.* The four were *The Beautiful Years* (1921), *Dandelion Days* (1922), *The Dream of Fair Women* (1924), and *The Pathway* (1928). As evocations of childhood and the countryside, they were of a high order. The North Devon coast was still unspoiled, and village life had not fundamentally altered since before the war. In my case I read *Dandelion Days* in my youth and was entranced with it; but in all four books atmosphere outweighed the quality of plot; and it was not until after the Second World War that he engaged on a mature series of fifteen novels, known collectively as *The Chronicle of Ancient Sunlight.*

The *Flax* novels did not sell well at first, but Williamson's financial situation was transformed when *Tarka the Otter* won the Hawthornden Prize of £100 in 1928. This not only made his name, but brought him immediate markets for his work, and incidentally provided him with the cash with which to buy a field at Ox's Cross above Georgeham, where he built a hermit's hut—a retreat for meditation and writing that he kept for the rest of his life, wherever his actual home. In fact it was not long before he and Loetitia—with a growing family—decided to move out of Georgeham into a long white cottage at Shallowford, near Castle Hill, the seat of the Fortescue family.

In terms of geography Williamson's stamping ground lay to the west and south-west of Exmoor proper, most of his Nature writing based upon observation of wild life outside the present National Park boundaries. The background of *Tarka,* for instance, was provided mostly by the river Taw, and that of *Salar* by the two rivers, Taw and Torridge. As Alan Jenkins pointed out, Williamson also relied on other sources of information, e.g. other books about otters: notably *Records of the Cheriton Otterhounds,* written by the Master of the Hunt, William Henry Rogers, to whom Williamson dedicated *Tarka,* and from whom he had received advice about errors in an article written earlier about an otter hunt down the river Lyn. There is no doubt too that Williamson made many forays into the heart of Exmoor, searching streams, watching birds and deer, and tramping the moorland. He commented *inter alia* on the growing commercialisation of the 'Doone Valley', evident even then. In general he was an acute observer with a good memory, rather than a trained naturalist; and he was able to write down what he had seen in language of sensitivity and imagination.

Of all his writings about the countryside, two works in particular concerned Exmoor. One was an early collection of wild life stories, *The Old Stag* (1926). The first of these, 'Stumberleap', told the tale of an old stag who, after an epic chase, swam across the Bristol Channel, taking half the hounds with him. The stag vanished but the hounds were drowned, their corpses washed up in Wales—a true incident from the past. This is a very good story indeed, skilfully told, with plenty of information about the behaviour of deer, harbouring, tufting, and the technique of the chase. The second work, *The Wild Red Deer of Exmoor,* was originally published as a pamphlet in 1931, and subtitled 'A Digression on the Logic and Ethics and Economics of Stag-Hunting in England Today'. It is not a coherent publication; but in it Williamson deploys the well-worn arguments for and against hunting, and simultaneously reveals his own ambivalence as sportsman and humanitarian. He demonstrated his approval of hunting on numerous occasions—as a follower of the otter hounds; by borrowing a mount from Violet Munnings (wife of the painter) to hunt with the 'D and S' in 1929; by fox hunting with a friend in Essex in the 1930s; and by a broadcast in 1936 in which he said:

> If I had the chance of being, say, a bullock in a pasture or a wild deer on the moor, I would choose to be a deer, so that when my turn came I would have a chance in the open instead of no choice in the confined horror of an abattoir.

In the early 1930s Williamson's fixation about the 1914 Christmas truce was inflated into admiration, and then idolisation, of Hitler. To quote Daniel Farson, author of *Henry—An Appreciation of Henry Williamson* (Michael Joseph, 1982), 'like most boys he could not resist the boom of the big parade'; and a visit to Berlin and then to the Nuremberg Rally in 1934 merely deepened his daze. He saw nothing in Nazi Germany but what he wanted to see, and the fact that he watched the Fuhrer from a nearby position in the crowd was fantasised into an actual exchange of words between the two men. Worse still, in the Foreword to the 1936 edition of *The Flax of Dream,* he wrote:

> I salute the great man across the Rhine, whose life symbol is a happy child.

This foolishness cost him dear, and he was never allowed to forget it. It led him to join the British Union of Fascists and attach himself to Oswald Mosley, and then—of all far-fetched fantasies—to campaign for the idea that T. E. Lawrence (another idol and, like Hitler, a non-smoker and non-drinker) should meet the Fuhrer and settle the peace of Europe. Whatever Lawrence thought about this, he was prevented from taking the matter further by losing his life in a motor cycle accident in 1935.

Williamson was labelled 'Fascist' or 'Bloody Fascist' for the rest of his life; and that may well have been the reason why he never received an Honour or other official recognition of his work—despite pressure behind the scenes from Kenneth Allsop, a latterday friend, and from myself when Secretary of the Royal Literary Fund. It also queered the pitch for him when he left Devon shortly before the Second World War and bought a 240-acre farm in Norfolk where—according to his book, *The Story of a Norfolk Farm* (Faber 1941)—he salved a derelict property and paid for the improvements by superhuman exertions on the ground and at his desk. Moreover he was received in the neighbourhood with a good deal of suspicion and, after the outbreak of war, was investigated by the local police, who sensibly wrote him off as a 'harmless eccentric'. Had it not been for Loetitia's calm support and for the many services she rendered in the village as President of the Women's Institute and much else, Williamson's situation might well have become impossible. As it was, his own character, innately awkward, frozen in adolescence by his experiences in the First World War, and tortured by the difficulties of farming in the Second, rendered him so difficult to live with that—after some twenty years of marriage—Loetitia divorced him. He then left East Anglia and returned to Ox's Cross to write the saga of Phillip Maddison in the fifteen titles that composed *A Chronicle of Ancient Sunlight.*

Williamson was lucky in his friendships. Had it not been for Malcolm Elwin, the critic and biographer, who lived at Putsborough Sands, a few miles from Georgeham, he might never have found a publisher for his new work. After Collins and Faber, his former publishers, had turned him down, he sent the first MS in the new series to Elwin who—thanks to an earlier introduction by Williamson—was acting as reader and adviser to the publishing house of Macdonald. Williamson had also, in 1946, contributed an article about Exmoor to the first issue of the *West Country Magazine,* which Elwin was then editing. The two men were therefore close friends and, in those days, Elwin thought highly of Williamson as a novelist, though he modified his opinions later. At all events he persuaded his colleagues at Macdonald to accept not only *The Dark Lantern* (1951), the initial title, but all of the fourteen that followed, culminating in the publication of *The Gale of the World* in 1969. This is not the place to try to assess the literary value of the work, beyond noting that—as publisher's editor—Elwin spent a great deal of time and effort cutting and streamlining Williamson's typescripts, always overloaded and over-written, until after the first half-dozen, the two men fell out. Nonetheless the series continued. However, as the reviewers observed, the quality of writing deteriorated, the novels becoming ever more autobiographical, many of the author's friends and enemies appearing in thinly disguised form.

In 1949 Williamson married Christine Duffield by whom he had one son, Harry, born in 1950. Christine had founded a P.N.E.U. school at Croyde and was running it with a friend. Henry approved and all went well for a time. Gradually however his writing habits and the accumulation of papers needed for the *Chronicle* forced him to buy a cottage in Capstone Place, Ilfracombe, and to hire a secretary to help him with the work and keep everything in order. Complications ensued, and the very burden of completing the *Chronicle* may have contributed to the onset of despair. Besides this Christine had to close her school when her partner left and, having thereafter to cope alone with her husband's temperament, problems piled up. She finally left him in 1962, went to teach at the village school in Exford, whence no amount of cajoling would bring her back. Williamson felt betrayed. In fact Christine left him, as Loetitia did, because she couldn't take any more.

Williamson's last years were sad. He spent more time at Ilfracombe—not an inspiring place for any writer—than he did at Ox's Cross, no longer a simple hut, but a heterogeneous collection of dwellings. A walk with Malcolm Muggeridge over The Chains—the gathering ground of many of Exmoor's rivers—and a good idea for a broadcast had to be cancelled. Williamson both missed his friends—he had alienated, among others, Tunnicliffe (illustrator of *Tarka*), Elwin, and for a time Allsop too—and yet found himself burdened by fan mail from all over the world. Despite several appearances on television, and valiant efforts by Allsop and Farson to present him on the screen and in print to the public, he waited in vain for literary recognition. But there was perhaps another factor—his buffoonery and boorishness at social gatherings of which I had personal experience when we met at West Country Writers' annual congresses, and once when he came to stay on my farm near Dulverton. He would resort to any kind of horseplay in order to draw attention to himself and dominate the conversation, which always rotated round his private woes and myths.

He died on 17 August 1977 and was buried at Georgeham. After his funeral, and the memorial service at St. Martin-in-the-Fields in the following December, some of his friends decided to contribute to a symposium, *Henry Williamson, The Man, The Writings* (Tabb House, 1980). This book, together with Farson's *Appreciation,* and Chapter 8 in Glen Cavaliero's *The Rural Tradition of the English Novel,* 1900-1939 (Macmillan, 1977) constitute—so far—the best group of guides to Williamson's complicated character and achievement as a writer.

ILFORD OLD AN

Pictures 1890 -

Introduction by Joyce Piggott

In February 1987 the first volume of Ilford Old and New went on sale. The response was most encouraging; it is nice to learn that our efforts are appreciated and that we are not alone in our interest of how things used to be. With this in mind we have decided to share with you a further selection of photographs exploring Ilford Old and New.

The route taken around Ilford follows that of Volume 1. On reaching the centre of Ilford, emphasis is placed on the old Ilford shops. A good few have long since disappeared, but their names will no doubt bring back memories to some readers. Other shops have stood the test of time and grown along with the town.

The location used for each of the present-day photographs is as close as possible to that of the original scene. This was not always easy to achieve, particularly in those areas of the town centre which have experienced alterations in road layout or the repositioning of buildings. Nevertheless, we feel that we have managed to capture the changes that have occured over the years.

Our grateful thanks to those readers who sent us several old photographs of the area; some of these have been included in this book. Thanks also to Mr. B. J. Page, who provides us with the fascinating historical notes.

ISBN 0 9512013 1 X

Ilford
July, 1987 ©

Fairlop Station, Forest Road, pictured in the late 1920's.
Opened to passengers in 1903. The site of the station was on land belonging to the Crown, who valued the site at £23,000.
The Great Eastern Railway offered £13,000 but finally agreed to an independent assessment of £15,763.
The last steam trains ran through Fairlop in 1947. In May 1948 the first Tube trains ran to Fairlop.
Below: the same view in 1987.

Mossford Green, looking towards Barkingside, pictured in the late 1920's.
The original School House is shown, which was built in 1842 (previously the school was held in a building in Horns Road).
The old National School was demolished in 1969. Site now occupied by Trinity Hall.
Below: the same view in 1987.

Tram Terminus, Barkingside about 1904.
Showing The Chequers and the original Police Station building, which was once a private house and was used as a Vicarage about 1851.
By 1861 the building was a beerhouse called the "Mossford Arms". The site became a Police Station again, as shown in the view below taken in 1987.

Tanners Lane, Barkingside about 1905.
In the area was once a Tannery, the site of which was probably "Tan Yard Farm", later known as "Red Rose Farm". This stood opposite the east end of Tanners Lane, site of Station Approach Road.
Below: the same view in 1982.

Dr. Barnardo's Church, Tanners Lane, Barkingside about 1904.
Known as the "Children's Church", and built in 1892.
Below: the same view in 1987.

Horns Road and The Horns Tavern, looking towards Barkingside. About 1905- 1910.
The name Horns is probably associated with the surname Horn(e) a name found in the area in the 16th and 17th century.
(Picture by courtesy of Mrs. M. Briggs).
Below: the same view in 1987.

Newbury Park Station about 1949.
The station was opened in 1903 by the Great Eastern Railway Company. The last steam trains left Newbury Park in November 1947 and in December of the same year the first tube trains arrived.
The present station was designed by Oliver Hill, 1949-50.
Below: the same view in 1983.

Ley Street, 1937.
The row of shops to the left of the picture includes a Bookbinders shop, newsagents and furniture upholsterer. The advertising sign on the right is for Oxcroft coals.
Tyne Hall, Ley Street, stood near Hainault Bridge. It was demolished in 1968.
Below: the same view in 1987.

Beehive Lane, junction of Cranbrook Road, about 1905.
Showing the entrance of Valentines Mansion.
The pillars and gates are now in Emerson Road.
Below: the same view in 1987.

Green's Stores, corner of Beehive Lane and Cranbrook Road, about 1920. Shops which traded in this area included, Poulter's Dairies, E.H. Butler Watchmaker, Vincent, Photographer and R. Henderson Baker. Below: the same view in 1987.

The Lodge and original Drive to Cranbrook Hall. About 1890.
The Cranbrook Castle Estate was developed, and houses were sold by Griggs Estate Agents in 1926. His office was at 1, Beehive Lane.
Below: the same view in 1987, showing the Valentine Telephone Exchange. The building of the exchange started in 1929.

Cranbrook Hall, shown before it was demolished in 1900.
The Cranbrook Estate was sold in 1897, for housing development. The Hall stood between 12 and 16 De Vere Gardens and 5 to 9 Endsleigh Gardens. Cranbrook Manor was one of the oldest that belonged to Barking Abbey.
Below: showing 12 to 16 De Vere Gardens in 1986.

E. Owen Clark and Son, Cranbrook Road, about 1930.
The business was established in 1928.
In recent years the premises were extended when the Jessie Norton Hat shop was acquired by Owen Clark.
(Picture by courtesy of Owen Clark)
Below: the shop in 1987.

G. J. Fairhead, Cranbrook Road, shown during a sale in 1954.
(Picture by courtesy of Fairheads).
Below: the same view in 1987, taken during the January sale.

W. Prentis and Company, 16 Cranbrook Road, pictured in 1924.
The famous "Ilford Cafe" is shown next door.
Prentis were greengrocers who also had other shops at 89 High Road, Ilford, 18 Cameron Road, Seven Kings and 10 Hainault Street.
Below: the same view in 1987. Cranbrook House, now known as "New Cranbrook House", was opened in 1924.

J. Senior, Confectioners and Bakers, Cranbrook Road, junction of York Road.
About 1900.
Below: the site now occupied by Lloyds Bank, shown in 1982.

Charles Pratt, Boot Repairer.
The picture shows the shop about 1917. The business started in 1910 at 1(A) Balfour Road. About 1937 the site was acquired by the National Westminster Bank and the business moved to 3, York Road.
Standing in the door of the shop is Mr. C. Pratt, the man in the cap is Mr. Harry Forrest who later had his own shoe repairers shop in High Street, Barkingside.
(Picture by courtesy of Mr. and Mrs. Forrest).
Below: the same view in 1987.

Junction of Balfour Road and Ley Street, about 1900.
The picture shows the site prior to the building of the Super Cinema (as shown on page 20 of "Ilford Old and New", volume one.
Below: view of the site shown in 1987.

Ilford Broadway, about 1907.
Showing the Clock Tower and the building now occupied by the National Westminster Bank.
Below: the same view, 1987, looking down Romford Road.

Ilford Broadway, about 1905.
Showing the Clock Tower and the White Horse Public House (site now occupied by Rosebys Ltd).
(Picture by courtesy of Miss M.G. King).
Below: the same view in 1987.

Ilford Lane, looking towards the Broadway, about 1908.
Below: the same view in 1987.

Ilford Lane, about 1890, showing the original "Hope" public house.
Below: showing the "Hope Revived" in 1987.

John Bodgers, High Road, Ilford, about 1913.
The business started at 113 High Road about 1890 in a single-fronted shop. The first store was known as "Manchester House".
Below: a view of the original site of the shops taken in 1987.

Moulton's High Road, Ilford, about 1910.
Below: showing Boots Chemists which occupies the site. 1987.

Ilford Hall. This photograph shows the site of the Hall, High Road, Ilford in 1900. The Hall was built about 1840 and demolished in 1901. The building was used by the old Ilford Urban District Council for meetings between 1898 and 1901.
Below: showing the site area of Ilford Hall, 1987.

Hainault Bridge, about 1890.
Known as Caucots Lane (1728) and later as Corkers Lane. The name Hainault Street was in use by the 1850's.
The Eastern Counties Railway built the Bridge between 1838-1839.
Below: Hainault Bridge, 1987.

Queens Terrace, High Road, Ilford about 1920.
The former Terrace was built about 1870 and the road opposite was Queens Road, which was built about 1880.
Below: showing the same area in 1987.

High Road, Seven Kings, looking towards Cameron Road, about 1905-1910.
The site of the Shannon Social Club was once the Seven Kings Cinema which opened in 1914.
Below: the same view in 1987.

High Road, Goodmayes, junction of Barley Lane, about 1905.
Goodmayes is mentioned in 1456, and said to be associated with the family of John Godemay (1319).
Below: the same view 1987.

Goodmayes Station, about 1910.
Opened in 1901. Like Seven Kings Station.
Goodmayes was built to serve the housing estates being erected by Cameron Corbett.
Below: the Station area 1987.

Chadwell Heath, High Road, about 1910.
John Norden's Map of Essex (1549) shows the spelling of the name as "Chawdwel".
In 1762 the King's Surveyor of Houses and Windows reported there were 13 houses in the area and 19 at Padnall Corner.
Below: a view of the same area in 1987.